THE SMALLEST SNOWMAN

By Sarah Fisch
Illustrated by Jim Durk

ISBN 0-439-81616-5

17 16 15 14 13   16 17 18 19/0

Designed by Michael Massen
Printed in the U.S.A.   40
First printing, January 2006

SCHOLASTIC INC.

New York   Toronto   London   Auckland   Sydney
Mexico City   New Delhi   Hong Kong   Buenos Aires

Winter's first big snowstorm had just begun. Tiny white flakes of snow swirled in the whooshing wind.

"There will be lots of snow to play in tomorrow, Clifford," Emily Elizabeth said.

The next morning, soft white snow blanketed the playground, the cars parked on the street, the trees, even the windowsill!

"It's so beautiful!" Emily Elizabeth sighed.

I can't wait to get out there and play! Clifford thought.

Emily and her friends pulled on their warm jackets, yanked on warm hats, and rushed outside to play.

Nina and Emily Elizabeth made beautiful snow angels. Other kids began building a snow fort to play in, and catching snowflakes on their tongues.

"How about a snowman contest?" Nina suggested.
"Let's see who can build the biggest!"
"YEAH!" the kids agreed.

Some ran inside to find old hats and scarves to add to their snowmen, while others started building. Each snowman was a little different, but which would be the biggest?

Everybody was excited, but Clifford the tiny red puppy was the most excited of all. *Building snowmen sounds fun!* he thought.

But the snow was quite deep in some places,
and Clifford had to hop very high with each step
to see where he was going. It was hard work!

All of a sudden, Clifford felt himself being turned over and over!

"Whoa!" one of the boys said. "This snowball has a tail!"

"And a face!" the other laughed.

"It's Clifford!" Emily cried, and took him to warm up in the laundry room with Mrs. Howard.

Clifford sighed. "I guess entering a snowman contest isn't for us little guys."

"Unless we built a small one," Lucy Sidarsky squeaked. "We could build one while the kids are inside eating lunch, just for fun."

"A small snowman is a great idea!" Clifford yelped. Lucy grinned. "I thought so," she said.

Clifford and Lucy got to work. Clifford pushed the snow with his nose. Lucy found yarn for the mouth and two buttons for eyes. Even Norville helped, bringing them two little twigs for arms.

"He's pretty small," Clifford said.
"He's pretty wonderful!" cried Lucy.
Norville laughed. "He's got a certain something,"
he admitted.

Back in the laundry room, Clifford and Lucy watched through the window to see if anybody noticed their special snowman.

"Look, they've spotted it!" Clifford whispered.

"Where did this little snowman come from?"
Emily Elizabeth asked.
"I don't know," Nina answered. "It wasn't
here before."

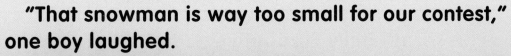

"That snowman is way too small for our contest," one boy laughed.

"I like his button eyes, though!" another boy said.

"Yeah, and I like his friendly smile!" chirped a little girl in braids.

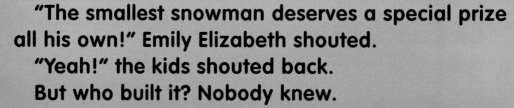

"The smallest snowman deserves a special prize all his own!" Emily Elizabeth shouted.
"Yeah!" the kids shouted back.
But who built it? Nobody knew.

Nobody except for Clifford and little Lucy Sidarsky, that is.

"Congratulations, Lucy!" said Clifford. "We're a great team!"

Sometimes being small isn't so bad!